RETURN OF THE
MAYA

Thus let it be done! Let the emptiness be filled!
Let the water recede and make a void,
Let the earth appear and become solid.
Let it be done.
Thus they spoke.
Let there be light, let there be dawn
in the sky and on the earth!
There shall be neither glory nor grandeur
in our creation and formation
until the human being is made, man is formed.
So they spoke.

—the creation of the world
from the Popol Vuh, the sacred book of the Maya

RETURN OF THE
MAYA

GUATEMALA—A TALE OF SURVIVAL

PHOTOGRAPHS BY
THOMAS HOEPKER / MAGNUM

HENRY HOLT AND COMPANY • NEW YORK

Henry Holt and Company, Inc.
Publishers since 1866
115 West 18th Street
New York, New York 10011

Henry Holt® is a registered trademark of
Henry Holt and Company, Inc.

Published in Canada by Fitzhenry & Whiteside Ltd.,
195 Allstate Parkway, Markham, Ontario L3R 4T8.
Originally published in Canada in 1998 by McClelland & Stewart, Inc.

Library of Congress Cataloging-in-Publication Data
Hoepker, Thomas.
Return of the Maya / photographs by Thomas Hoepker.—1st American ed.
p.   cm.
ISBN 0-8050-6007-3 (hardbound: alk. paper)
1. Mayas—Social conditions. 2. Mayas—Government relations. 3. Forensic
anthropology—Guatemala. 4. Genocide—Guatemala. 5. Guatemala—Politics
and government. 6. Guatemala—Social life and customs. I. Title.
F1435.3.S68H64   1998
305.897'4152—dc21   98-20081

Henry Holt books are available for special promotions and
premiums. For details contact: Director, Special Markets.

First American Edition 1998

Designed by Susanne Baumgartner

Printed in Hong Kong
All first editions are printed on acid-free paper.∞

1 3 5 7 9 10 8 6 4 2

CONTENTS

Rigoberta Menchú-Tum was awarded the Nobel Peace Prize in 1992. She grew up in a village in the Quiché region, where her father, her mother, and her brother were brutally killed by the Guatemalan army. She has been a political and spiritual force for the Maya all her life. We met Ms. Menchú-Tum in the house of her husband, in the village of San Pedro Jocopilas, and we asked her what, if anything, the peace accords have brought to the Maya.

"Well, I think there's been enormous progress: Progress at the local political level and in the civic committees. Progress especially in participation during the two elections we've just gone through. Our people have done a huge job to try to empower women. For many years there was no such thing as a women's electoral group. A lot has been accomplished in the recent past.

"But we are far from having solved all the problems yet, especially those of misery, hunger, and poverty. The civil war, which lasted thirty-six years, may not have been the only reason why there are no hospitals, no medical centers, no job opportunity in most rural areas. The armed conflict was being used by the government as a pretext for the reluctance to develop the countryside.

"Extremely cruel methods were used against the indigenous educators in Guatemala, who granted the continuity of a culture which was so deep and so rich. Many of them were old and represented very strong local leadership. They were also good community organizers. The counterinsurgents went after precisely these wise men and women, so as to kill off the local leaders, like my father. I also think there's still racism at all levels. There's a constant underrating, pointing fingers and making the natives look ridiculous whenever they're included in joint actions with the nonnatives. As an example, you won't find a native at a reception in the capital city where matters of importance are discussed and negotiated. Right here in San Pedro Jocopilas, when we came here for the first time in 1994, we wouldn't even walk in the streets because we were afraid. Why? Because so many people had been killed in this town. Right here at the corner, near the house we just passed, they carted people away on trucks and killed them. In the San Pedro cemetery there are secret mass graves, and the murderers still live here.

A TALK WITH RIGOBERTA

"But things are starting to open up little by little, and now, well, we feel somewhat calmer. In the village we've noticed that even natives and ladinos do a lot of things together. In sum: The peace agreements are very important. But they are only political agreements. We still have a long way to go before they're implemented to bring about the reforms we are so eager for.

"I also think it's time to let the villages arrange their lifestyles for themselves. There's been a perfectionist, paternalistic attitude toward Mayans wearing jeans and T-shirts. One thing is for sure: Native dress does not make you a native. It's only one aspect of our very comprehensive culture which is based on community values. Those values have not been destroyed; this fills us with great pride. We have to promote self-respect and pride, above all among our women, who should not be excluded from managing anything that exists in the world today.

"What makes us strong is the continuity of thought and spirituality, the experience of our grandparents, and a lot of mysterious things that aren't being talked about and never will be. We have a certain mysticism about life, our own way of praying, of thinking, of living. Our old people had a lot to do with this life, and they suddenly killed them. But they couldn't eliminate the Maya way of being. This is a lifelong thing, right?

"Two family members were murdered in this very house. It happened in almost every house you visit. Digging out the dead from mass graves inflicts a pain on the relatives that nobody can relieve. Nobody who hasn't lived through it will ever understand it. It's a horrifying truth. It's our truth. It's our historical memory. Ignoring the truth is an attitude that has to be fought. But then again, it's more than just a painful past; it has consequences as well. There is less tranquillity in the villages now, more thefts and robberies and more violence. This climate did not exist before.

"Our dead need to be treated very solemnly. When the loved ones are not buried with dignity in a proper graveyard, our people will spend generations searching for them. So the murderers' guilt will not expire over time. Not one of the murderers has been convicted so far. We haven't even managed to get a trial, not even a trial for the massacre of four hundred native people at Xamán in 1995. Yes, the Xamán killers are in prison, but after the three years the case has been going on people realize that walking through the mazes of justice is not only an act of faith but a never-ending job. We begin to realize that justice is expensive, and since all the victims are poor, we'll never achieve justice.

"The process of recovering our historical memory was like a healing, and everybody knew that. What they didn't know was how many names there were, the enormous number of people responsible for the 1.4 million cases of human-rights violations which are documented in the REMHI report. The recent murder of Bishop Juan Gerardi, who had compiled that report, was a horrible political crime. It's like a message to all of us, and we've gotten the message.

"When people ask me whether I could imagine myself in some political office, I say no, that's not my role. I'm involved in social issues, I'm the voice of the conscience like lots of other people. Some day I'd like to see the Maya respected. Rather than become president of Guatemala, I'd like to be able to grant five thousand or ten thousand scholarships to native professionals who did not complete their university studies. I don't believe that you can do that by joining a political party.

"This millennium should be the platform for raising the respect for native peoples, not just here in Guatemala, but throughout the world. I think many of my brothers and sisters are fit to become president. But what we need is not a native president; what we need is an impact with regard to par-

ticipation, schooling, training, and opportunities, so that we can constitute good municipal governments. Being a native doesn't make you a good mayor. You also need administrative capabilities, a working plan, and priorities. I would be bored living in Guatemala City.

I'm very happy living right here in the countryside. Sometimes I go to San Pedro; sometimes I go to my birthplace of Chimel, or Uspantán. I'd be very bored in an office in Guatemala City. My father's land is beautiful. It's got a lot of water. A cloudy rain forest, which is the focus of a lot of veneration and solemnity. Whenever I want a spiritual retreat from everything, I go there. For the Expo 2000 in Hannover I'm organizing a beautiful pavilion that will be worthy of the native people. I don't want a paternalistic folklore racist pavilion. I want to present the progress we made. Our achievements. The greatness of our cultures and of our people. So I don't feel bad for the Maya people. They'll keep on living just like they've been doing for thousands of years, for many thousands of years to come."

The year is 1839. John Lloyd Stephens, the famed travel writer from New York, and his companion, the English draftsman Frederick Catherwood, had made the exhausting trip to the as yet unexplored Maya ruins of Copán deep in the rain forest of Honduras. "The city was desolate," Stephens writes, describing his first impression. "It lay before us like a shattered bark in the midst of the ocean, her masts gone, her name effaced, her crew perished, and none to tell whence she came, to whom she belonged, how long on her voyage, or what caused her destruction." The explorers found, scattered amid the thick brush, embraced by the roots of giant trees, all the splendor of an ancient metropolis: towering pyramids, elaborate chiseled stelae with menacing portraits of rulers, and miles of strange and beautiful hieroglyphic text carved in stone. But nothing stirred, except some monkeys and parrots high in the trees. "Who were the people that built this city?" asks Stephens. "America, say historians, was peopled by savages; but savages never reared these structures, savages never carved these stones. We asked the Indians who made them, and their dull answer was 'Quien sabe?' 'Who knows?'"

Speculation about the ruined wonders of Mesoamerica and their builders had been rife through the centuries. Some earlier travelers had stated that Arabs or Egyptians must have built the abandoned cities. The Austrian adventurer Count Waldeck had credited the Chaldeans, the Phoenicians, and even the "Hindoos." But hardly anyone thought for a moment that the shy brown people who still inhabited the woods around the ruins might actually be the descendants of the ancient Maya, the great-grandsons and -daughters of mighty warlords, of the priests, the astronomers, the scribes, and the artisans who had created one of the greatest civilizations in history.

Certainly it had never crossed the minds of Spanish conquistadores that those "stinking godless Indian devils" might somehow be related to the enlightened society that must have inhabited these cities of old. In fact the conquerors did not care too much about any ruins—there were no precious metals to be found, nothing but carved stones. And the mercenaries had their hands full anyway, subjugating the barbarians and transforming them into obedient subjects of the Spanish monarch. And the priests had to work hard to make good Christians out of ignorant pagans. One of them, the theologian Juan de Sepúlveda, summarized the prevailing ideology nicely for the court in Seville: "Indians are inferior to the Spanish just as children are to adults, as women are to men and, let's face it, as apes are to men."

THE LOST TRIBES

An Introduction

Sepúlveda's antagonist, the courageous bishop of Chiapas, Bartolomé de las Casas, wrote his controversial eyewitness account of the first modern holocaust in 1552. His book *The Devastation of the Indies* is a tale of unspeakable greed, arrogance, and horror. Las Casas writes about men, women, and children being enslaved or tortured, some burned alive "thirteen at a time in memory of Our Redeemer and his twelve apostles." About the populous province of Guatemala he writes: "Spaniards have slain four or five million souls in fifteen or sixteen years from the year twenty-four to the year forty. And they will go on killing." He describes butcher shops that sold human flesh as dog food, "where the corpses of Indians are hung up, on display, and someone will come in and say, 'Give me a quarter of that rascal there.'" Las Casas became the first Spaniard to see the Indians as human beings, arguing that they should be entitled to what we today would call "human rights."

Another man of the cloth, Fra Diego de Landa, is the author of a different but equally remarkable book. His account *Yucatan Before and After the Conquest* is such a detailed description of the life, the customs and costumes, the religion and myths, and the complex calendar and highly sophisticated astronomy of the natives that it has been described to be the foundation of 99 percent of what we know about the Maya today. However, his deep admiration of indigenous society and culture did not stop de Landa from performing his religious duties. In the infamous auto-da-fé at Maní he destroyed five thousand Maya idols and twenty-seven of their hieroglyphic books: "Since they contained nothing but superstition and falsehoods of the devil, we burned them all, which they took most grievously, and which gave them great pain." It has been estimated that ninety-nine times as much knowledge of Maya history, art, and sciences as were contained in de Landa's famous book went up in smoke on that dark day in 1562.

So strong was the fervor of these conquistadores of the soul that it was not enough for them merely to subjugate, maim, or kill a foreign race. They also wanted to erase every evidence of Maya civilization, a case not just of genocide but of attempted culturecide. Severed from their roots, the Maya were, in fact, reduced to the level of mindless animals, and that in turn lent moral justification to their tormentors: Why not kill them like wild dogs?

This attitude toward the Maya, no doubt, has survived the centuries. Until recently indígenas were not allowed to perform their own complex religious rites but had to pretend to be devout Catholics. To be sure, they did keep their beliefs alive, but they had to hide their sacred idols and their altars in caves or on remote mountains. Most indígenas of Guatemala are not aware of their descent from the ancient Maya. An Indian child who went to school in Guatemala had to learn a foreign language, Spanish, before he or she could start to practice reading, writing, or math. No indígenas could be sure to get justice in the courts unless they spoke Spanish or could pay an interpreter. Most of the time the natives lost out to the ladinos in the frequent land disputes; this in a country where roughly 2 percent of the population owns 70 percent of the land.

For a moment it had seemed that things might take a turn for the better in 1951, when Jacobo Arbenz was elected president of Guatemala in a landslide vote. Arbenz, a mildly liberal colonel, had promised democratic progress and land reform, and indeed he went ahead and expropriated land from the big owners, among them the American United Fruit Company. But United Fruit knew quite well how to play the anticommunist cards at home and in the media and, lo and behold, two years later President Eisenhower agreed to a devious CIA plot to remove Arbenz from power. With the democratically elected government disposed of, a military junta was installed with America's blessings. United Fruit was given back its land plus an $11 million tax windfall as consolation, and the repression of the Maya population continued.

To nobody's surprise, guerrilla groups began to set up camp in remote jungle regions. And, of course, the military reacted with force and terror. Most of the ethnic cleansing was directed at the Maya, who were thought to be sympathizers of the Communist rebels. The United States sent large shipments of weapons and army trainers. By 1981, death-squad killings of thirty-five to forty people a day were reported. Most of the massacred indígenas showed signs of torture. The heritage of the conquistadores had resurfaced in the modern Guatemalan army. Again the Indians were denounced as animals and vermin; again any hint of an indigenous high culture was suppressed.

Yuri Valentinovich Knorosov, a mild-mannered Russian ethnologist, had been instrumental in deciphering the Maya code, the ancient hieroglyphs that had so long been an enigma to science. Knorosov had to do all his theoretical work from books and papers in faraway Leningrad since he was never permitted to leave the Soviet Union for the lands of the Maya. Finally in 1990 perestroika allowed him to come to Guatemala, and for the first time he could touch the cryptic stones he knew so well. Then one night in Guatemala City a phone rang in Knorosov's room. "Leave Guatemala within seventy-two hours or be killed," said the male voice. The death squads had caught up with the scholar who had given a voice to the ancient Maya, who had proven that the Indians had a literary culture older than that of the Spanish.

Six years later: a new beginning, another hope. Finally the Guatemalan government has made peace with the rebels. After thirty-six years the longest civil war in Latin America has come to an end on December 29, 1996. There will also be new laws and human rights for the Maya after five hundred dark years. They will be equal citizens, they may freely practice their religion, they may officially use their languages, the courts will be bilingual, there will be democracy for all—so they say.

RETURN OF THE
MAYA

Beauty is a basic necessity for the Maya, just like food and drink.
Beauty is chiseled into ancient stones, woven
into their garments, displayed in markets,
and becomes part of every celebration.

TOILS AND BEAUTY

Thursdays and Sundays are market days in the mystical town of Chichicastenango. Families walk for hours to bring flowers and vegetables, which they arrange with great care around the sacred steps of the church of Santo Tomás.

Once a week peasants come to the animal market of San Francisco El Alto in the cool morning fog that is so frequent in the Guatemalan highlands. Some walk barefoot; all walk for hours. Most return home with a pittance of profit.

The famous woolen garments are still being woven and worn by Maya women. Each region has its distinct patterns and colors. Much of that tradition was lost in the civil war. because the peasants feared that if they could be identified by their dress as belonging to a guerrilla area. their lives would be in danger.

The weaver of Santiago
Atitlán wears the local hat
made of red ribbons wound
around her head. Most Maya
smell like smoked meat
because they live with a
permanent wood fire in their
homes. It is needed for
cooking and to keep
everybody warm in the
bone-chilling nights of the
highlands.

After the July rains the hills of the Quiché region turn green and lush. Corn is planted on terraces that have been hacked into the slopes by generations. The cycle of maize planting and harvesting determines the rhythm of indigenous life.

The naïve beauty of the church at San Andrés Xequl is an example of Maya craft, just as is the elaborate handwoven *huipil* blouse worn by a girl in the town of Chajul in northern Quiché.

Mornings are cool in the town of Nebaj. In every community in Guatemala the old Catholic church, built by the Spanish power in the main square, marks the center of colonial and spiritual dominance.

17

The women of
San Andrés Sajcabajá
wear elaborate
headdresses of
pompoms and silver
nets in church. The
landscape of the
highlands, with
picture-book volcanoes
surrounding Lake
Atitlán, provides a
panorama of grandeur
and beauty.

The vegetables in the market at Almolonga near Quezaltenango must be among the largest in the world. Volcanic activity in the region heats the soil, transforming the area into a giant hothouse that yields a constant harvest all year round.

The beauty of
market scenes
can conceal
the hardship
and struggle of
daily life in the
villages. Children
grow up early.
A life of hard
work lies ahead.

Simple beauty lies
in the details of
a market stand in
Chichicastenango.
The flower petals
are taken by
worshipers to the
church of Santo
Tomás, where
they will please
and appease
the saints.

Sixteen years after her husband and two sons were executed by government troops, Albina Tzoy has found the rotting remains of her family in a shallow grave in a cornfield near El Tabil, Quiché.

Digging into the earth to uncover the dead means digging into an ugly past and digging into the lives of the survivors as well.

DARK SECRETS

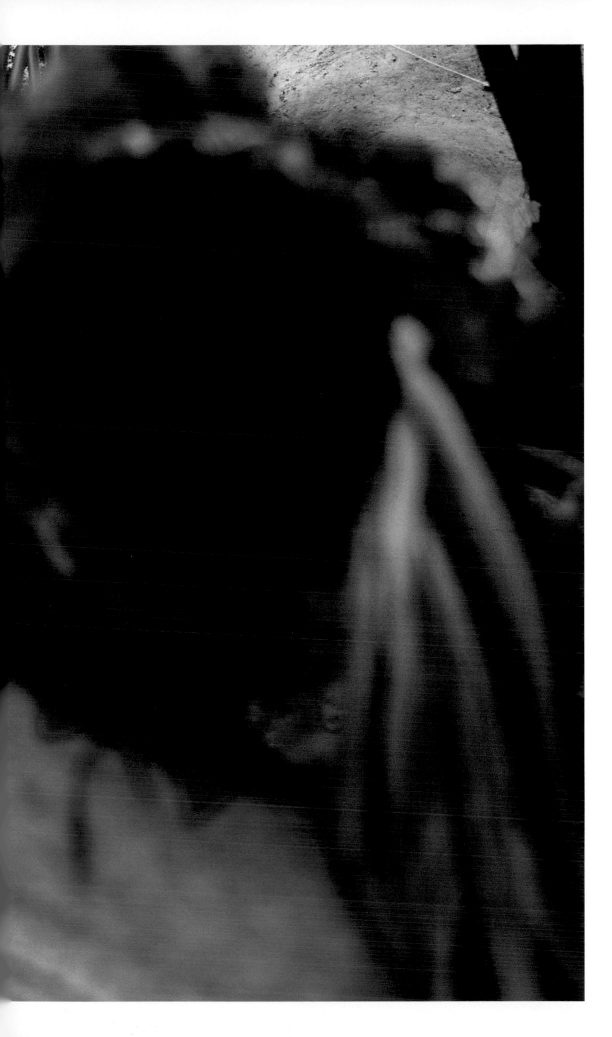

Five skeletons are being unearthed in the cloister garden at San Andrés Sajcabajá. The church grounds had been used as a military torture center in the 1980s. A widow watches in silence.

Anthropologists have
exhumed and cleaned
three skeletons of
war victims. A rubber
sandal becomes
visible between two
skulls. Identification
numbers mark
the bodies and
information about
the site is displayed
on a blackboard
for the official
photographs.

Full of horror and curiosity, these women watch as a team of
anthropologists digs up the remains of the men in their family.
The wives had been present when their husbands were shot to death
in a cornfield in 1981, but they never dared to request a proper burial
during the time of military rule.

Kneeling next
to three exhumed
skeletons, a family
mourns their dead.
The local Maya
priest has decorated
the corpses with
candles and flowers
and now performs
an elaborate
ceremony that
will finally put
the victims to a
proper rest.

In the ruined church
of San Andrés Sajcabajá
a big Mayan ceremony
for the dead is performed
by a group of local priests.
Flowers have been
arranged in a circle around
the holy fire. Many victims
had been hastily buried
under the floor of the
church by their
military torturers.

THE OTHER KILLING FIELDS

After the July rains, the valley glistens fresh and green. The cornstalks are almost as tall as a man. Toward the north, the mountain ranges of the Quiché blur into infinity. Four men dressed in traditional white Indian garb are hacking away in the bean field below. Children laugh. Roosters crow. Blue smoke wafts from a house—the lunchtime tortillas are on the hearth. A peaceful image?

At the end of the valley, in San Andrés Sajcabajá, a town of two thousand souls, they are searching for 492 corpses. Padre Santos, the young parish priest, has stored the names neatly in his Toshiba laptop: Marino Chach, Domingo Choc, Andrés Choc Chach, Joseterio Yac, Catalina Yac, María Ixcuna. . . . These are the names of parishioners; people who were shot, slain, strangled, tortured, or burned; or those who have simply disappeared during the thirty-six years of civil war—mainly during what the locals call *La Violencia*, those particularly horrible years between 1978 and 1983. Now a peace treaty has been signed between the conservative Arzú government and the leftist guerrilla fighters of the URNG. The Maya, who make up 60 percent of the population, are now finally acknowledged as full-fledged citizens. They now have human rights, they are being told, just like the ladinos, the Spanish-speaking upper class. All of a sudden, they are being told that even the military are their friends, that troops are to be reduced by one third, and that the rebels from the mountains have surrendered their weapons to the UN.

Padre Santos does not need to go far in his search for war victims. Whenever he leaves his church these days to use the latrine in the cloister garden, he has to walk around a ditch six feet deep. Forensic anthropologists from Guatemala City are scraping five skeletons out of the dirt down below. Slowly a skull becomes visible, then shreds of clothing, a multicolored, woven Indian satchel bag, and rubber sandals made of automobile tires such as the poor people around here wear. Women and children, dressed in the magnificent traditional costumes of San Andrés, the black-yellow-and-red woven skirts, the embroidered *huipil* blouses, and the headdresses made of metallic silver netting, are hunkering at the upper edge of the grave. They speak softly and sparingly, gazing down with a mixture of horror, suspense, and mourning. They sit quietly and patiently for a very long time.

Down below, Leonel Paiz and Reinaldo Azevedo are ankle-deep in the mud, shoveling, scraping, and brushing methodically, peeling bones out of the earth—a hip, some ribs, an arm. Leonel and Reinaldo had studied anthropology in the hopes of excavating thousand-year-old Maya temples in the lowlands. Now they are excavating the Maya themselves, corpses lying in the earth for no more than twelve to fifteen years, victims of unspeakable violence, people with names, people with survivors.

According to Fernando Moscoso Möller, the director of the Institute of Forensic Anthropology in the capital, "Initially people estimated that there were four hundred clandestine cemeteries in the entire country from the time of *La Violencia*. But that seems absurd now; there are many many more, and news of new graves arrives every day. This is the horrible result of a systematic policy of ethnic cleansing." Official reports cite 150,000 people killed during the civil war and 50,000 missing, but nobody knows if these figures are accurate. They should be checked, grave by grave, skeleton by skeleton. But there are no funds in the national budget earmarked for this task. The salaries of the forensic anthropologists are paid from foreign donations.

When "Individual SAQ 1-2-2" was still alive, probably no one ever paid him such careful attention as Leonel Paiz is doing now, precisely cleaning and lining up six ribs on a board in the ditch. His colleague reads out what he has just entered on his form: "Two left ribs broken, one missing. A cloth band around Individual SAQ 1-2-1's eyes. A belt around the cervical vertebrae of Individual SAQ 1-2-3." (Strangulation cannot be clearly proven by examining bones.) Reinaldo has labeled brown paper bags with a felt tip pen "lower left extremities," "head and jawbone," or "right hand." An average skeleton requires seventeen bags. The bags go into a cardboard box, which is sent to the capital for identification.

√ "There were battles here in 1980 between the guerrilla fighters and the army," Padre Santos explains. "Of all places, the military picked our church and the cloister garden, and turned them into their torture center." The people of San Andrés Sajcabajá had a hunch about what was going on behind the cloister wall. Men were arrested in the street and dragged into the church; women disappeared without a trace. Often screams were heard from the church, and occasionally smoke came out of the roof at night. The stench was nauseating. The Quiché Maya kept their heads down. Whenever they passed the church carrying their heavy burdens, they quickened their pace. They always tried to keep a low profile. Some unfortunate people had a high profile, such as those who owed money to Don Polo the cattle dealer, who was merciless and had friends in the military; such as those who had gone to school and spoke a little Spanish, as they might wonder about things or even be Commu-

Anthropologist Leonel Paiz meticulously cleans a skull with a fine brush. He has studied Maya archaeology, but recently he took a course in forensic medicine. Years of hard and dirty work lie ahead of him.

nists; such as those who had a little bit more than everybody else, like Pedro Moreno the store owner, since he had stuff in his *tienda* worth being looted.

Domingo Aj Choc boosted his courage with a few drinks before coming to the cloister. He himself had been a prisoner in this garden in 1982. "*Gracias a Dios*, they let me go," he mumbles. Because he is drunk on sugarcane booze and his Spanish is very limited, we have to repeat many questions and later rewind the tape several times in order to understand what he was trying to say. "They locked me up in that shed over there. There was so much blood! It looked awful! And they had strung up two men there by their arms. One of them had lasted four days and nights. The other one was still alive. 'So you don't wanna die?' the soldiers said to him. 'Okay, so now you can go dig a latrine for us, twelve feet deep, twelve feet long,' they said to him. They kept me here for fifteen days. I was tied up all the time. Like a goat. They gave me nothing to eat and no water. Once they gave us gnawed-up rinds of watermelon. I sucked them completely dry. And Polo Reyes, the military commissioner, said, 'Spit it out! You finally gonna tell us where the weapons are hidden? What are the names of your Communist friends?' I said, 'I don't know people like that. Don Polo, you're my *patrón*, I always did good work for you, and now you're

The colonial church of San Andrés Sajcabajá was the scene of unspeakable horrors after the military installed a torture center here in 1980.

treating me like this!' I almost starved to death. Finally they gave me some broth, *caldo de gente*." What kind of broth? "*Caldo de gente*," Domingo repeats. "They boiled human flesh. Because they had cut these people into pieces. What was I supposed to do? I wanted to stay alive."

We hear a scream coming from the ditch behind us. A woman is pointing down: "That's my husband's shirt, the yellow shirt. That's what he was wearing when they took him away." Francisca Toj Chach sends her daughter to the store to buy candles; then she is helped down into the grave. She lights three candles next to the yellow scrap of cloth and the bones that may once have been Vicente Chach. "They dumped him in this ditch like a bundle. He can't defend himself anymore. Now I have to fight for him," Francisca says. "The murderers are rich ladinos. They haven't a care in the world, not like us poor *naturales*. I see them on the street, and my heart knows that they have done this deed. I keep my mouth shut. I'm all alone with eight children. Who gives the orders in our house now? Just me, never anyone but me!"

The anthropologists stop working when the candles have burned down. Later they will analyze the remains from Grave 1-2 in the laboratory, comparing the findings in the computer with the evidence gleaned from their interviews with the women. "Was your husband right-handed? Was he missing any teeth?" they had asked. "Did your son have a broken bone or an injury? What was he wearing when they came for him?" Francisca Toj Chach's chances to gain certainty about her husband are not all that great. By the middle of 1997 the chronically understaffed Forensic Anthropology Foundation had examined 29 secret cemeteries in Guatemala; they had found 431 corpses, 89 of which could be identified. An excerpt from their matter-of-fact list of horrors reads as follows: Chichupac, Rabinal: 32 victims, 7 identified; Río Negro, Rabinal: 177 victims (including 100 children), 3 identified; Cuarto Pueblo, Ixcán: 300 victims, totally charred remains, 0 identified. Sometimes identification of the remains is easy, like in a lush cornfield near the village of El Tabil. A group of young Catholic anthropologists is digging here for the victims of a massacre. Unlike at San Andrés, they know exactly where to look, since many people had been watching when the soldiers came on April 17, 1982.

The killings in the cornfields were well organized and were part of the *tierra quemada* operation, the scorched-earth policy that completely obliterated 440 highland villages. They came with a list of men's names and called out 18 of them; they shot them all on the spot and immediately buried them in shallow graves in the field. All these years the women knew exactly where their husbands were lying, but they did not dare talk about it or dig them up for a proper burial. So they plowed the field and sowed the corn above the dead for sixteen summers. They harvested and waited, and then plowed and sowed anew. And now it was finally time for the dead men to come out of the earth. Three of them, no less, belonged to Albina Tzoy: her husband, who had been thirty-nine at the time, and her two sons, aged thirteen and nineteen; three skeletons dressed in pants, shirts, and shoes. When the anthropologists were finished, once all the measurements and all the photographs had been taken, the local Maya priest Agustín Chuck Ajaw arrived. Within a few minutes, he transformed the gruesome tableau of death into a beautiful, solemn, and dignified image of candles, flowers, petals, and incense. Then he officiated a Maya Mass for the Dead. Albina Tzoy, the widow, and two of her relatives knelt down next to the bones, sobbing and holding candles. Finally, things fell into place for the survivors: Finally the dead men got the ceremony they were entitled to, and finally there was proper mourning and closure.

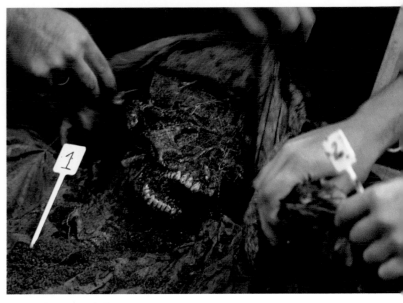

Remnants of torture victims and their belongings were dug up from under the church's floor. The building itself was severely damaged in an earthquake.

Three skeletons with scraps of clothes and a Mayan woven bag were found in this grave by Reinaldo Azevedo, who carefully registers all details about the find. Evidence about Guatemala's recent past is being gathered in a professional way, but only a few victims can be identified.

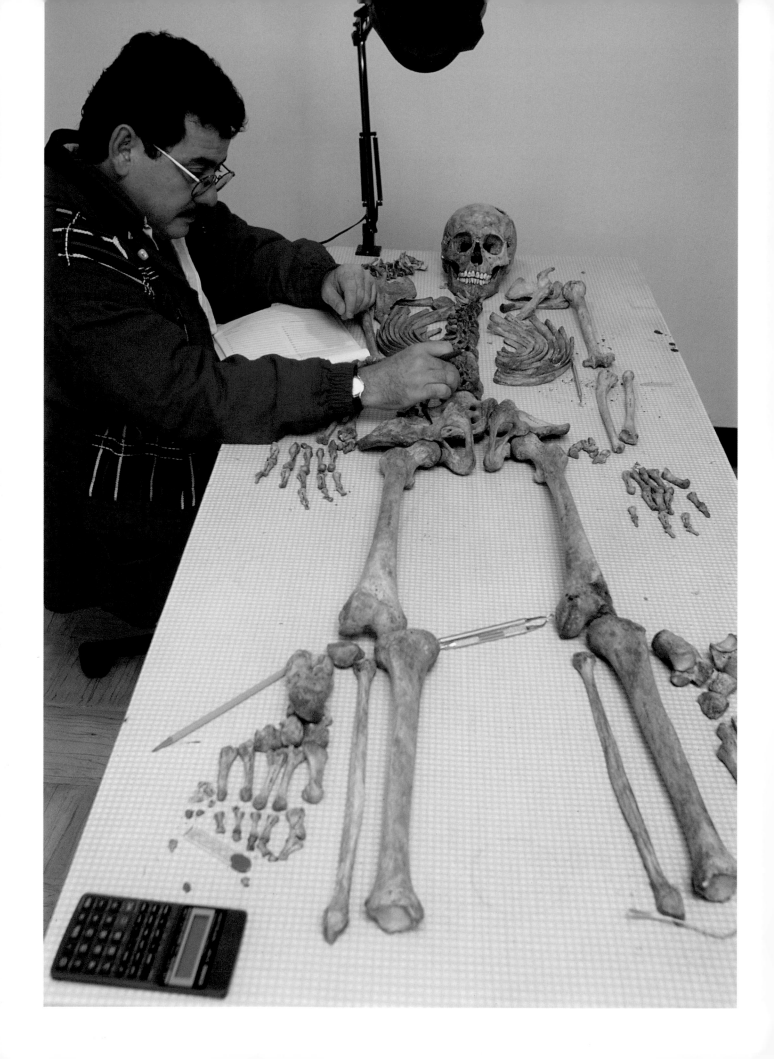

Skeletons of war victims are being reassembled in the Institute of Forensic Anthropology in Guatemala City. If identification is made, the remains will be returned to their families. The carpenter Jorge Cherec in Chimaltenango specializes in making small coffins for the burial of bones. Widows in Xeatzán Bajo visit the graves of their murdered husbands once a week.

45

Jacinta Tzog was there when Cándido Noriega arrived with soldiers at the *finca* of Tululché at five o'clock in the morning of November 22, 1982. She watched from a distance as he selected ten men and ordered them murdered with clubs, rifle butts, and machetes. "They poured gasoline on my father in his house and set him on fire. Only his two feet were left when we came back. They killed

THE VICTIM

my husband and my brother. I had to watch. I was there." She saw Noriega rape women and heard him order to hang other men. "I knew Don Cándido well, he had a few years earlier worked as a manager at Tululché where I lived with my family. They took cattle away and they also burned the woods. They said that *guerrilleros* lived there. But that was not true. We never had any rebels in Tululché."

Twenty-seven witnesses have testified against Noriega in his first trial, all of them Quiché Indians: twenty-two women and five men who had been present on that fateful morning in 1982. They told their stories to the court haltingly, with only a single interpreter there to translate from Quiché into Spanish. And the judge, Don Olegario Labbé, had mostly slept through the proceedings—everyone who was there said so. But despite his napping, the judge made note of many contradictions in the witnesses' statements regarding certain times and dates—as if every Maya had a watch and kept a diary. Furthermore, they had all feared for their lives at that time, and still feared for it. At any rate, the accused, Cándido Noriega, was acquitted after a trial lasting only four days, and everybody in Tululché was very frightened because Noriega had threatened to poison their drinking water. "Don Cándido has many friends here, even today," says Jacinta. "It cannot be that he is set free. We want him punished. He has caused so much suffering." How justice and atonement are handled in Guatemala is the subject of an astonishingly honest explanation by Amilcar Méndez, member of parliament of the Democratic Front for the province of Quiché: "In our country the courts are in the habit of deciding their cases not in accordance with the law, but in accordance with the amount of the bribe. The Noriega case is just one example."

Cándido Noriega, allegedly the worst war criminal of Guatemala, is charged with having violated human rights in 156 cases during the 1980s: 35 murders, 44 kidnappings, 14 rapes, 21 grand larcenies, 7 instances of arson, 6 of bodily injury, and 6 of blackmail, as well as 23 illegal arrests. We meet Noriega in the historic municipal jail of Santa Cruz de Quiché right next to the cathedral. The guard at the door has no objections to our visit, and very soon there he is, standing in front of us in his big sombrero, black beard, and pointed cowboy boots. Noriega's first trial is already behind him. "Nothing but slander," he says. "First they gave me freedom, but then they filed an appeal, and now there's supposed to be another trial—unbelievable." Noriega sits very straight on a bench, facing us, in the entrance hall to the jail. A garish wall painting of a forgiving Jesus is behind his back, and under that image is a bored policeman with a typewriter. The barred door leading to the street is conspicuously ajar. "First there were only ten crimes, now it's supposed to be more than one hundred fifty! Do I really look like that kind of a person? All the witnesses are lying. Some of them accuse me of having raped them. I don't need these women. We've got plenty of our own for stuff like that. Love isn't a competition with rams, bulls, or stallions. That was a dirty war. These people killed each other. I've no idea why. I'm a very honorable person. I like to work clean. The peace treaty has brought us nothing," Noriega underscores. "There are more thieves than ever. I can see that now, since I'm in here. And every day you hear about kidnappings on the street. This didn't happen in the old days, things were healthier then."

THE VILLAIN

But why, then, is he being charged with all these crimes? "Because some people think it's very nice to take 2,240 hectares of land away from me for only $1,035! That's my land in Tululché. It's worth at least a million dollars nowadays. The archdiocese is behind all that. They want to take away my land. Even though they're Catholics!" As is so often the case in Latin America, all this bloodshed was basically rooted in a land dispute. And so it seems that like so many others, Noriega tried to take advantage of the war in order to get rich. He saw a chance to grab the big beautiful *finca* of Tululché for himself by murdering or expelling the Indians who had settled there. At the time he was a civilian army commissioner, which meant that he had power and he had guns.

A simple memorial to the Mayan holocaust has been built by parishioners in the church of Nebaj. Wooden crosses in memory of locals who were killed or have disappeared are left under a poignant altar painting.

Peace in Guatemala has brought religious freedom
to the Maya for the first time in five hundred years.
Now they worship at their own altars,
pray to their own gods.

BACK TO THE GODS

This is a new beginning, a time of hope. They have tried to steal our religion from us for the past five hundred years but we never gave up. Now, finally, we can worship our gods in the open—for all to see." The man who explains this is an authority on Maya religion. Cirilo Pérez Oxlaj, or *Lobo Errante*, the Wandering Wolf, is a member of the Council of Elders of the Maya priesthood. Cirilo lives on a large farm in a lovely valley near San Francisco El Alto with his dignified wife, many children, and innumerable grandchildren. But these days he is home only occasionally. "I don't quite understand it myself, but now that there is peace, I always seem to be on an airplane—to South America, Europe, North America. There are indigenous conferences and meetings everywhere. I never have to pay anything. Beautiful hotels, big cities, halls filled to capacity—it's almost too much for me." This well-traveled man would much prefer to spend more time in his homeland, in nature, which is so important to him and which he wants to protect for his grandchildren.

Cirilo has the power to ordain new priests and train them in his religion's complex rites and rules, which date back three millennia. Becoming a Maya priest is a cumbersome procedure. The candidates have to visit thirteen altars throughout the country. They are set in secret locations—on mountaintops, in the forest, at holy lakes, inside caves, or near waterfalls. To reach them you have to hike long distances, climb up steep slopes, or rappel down on ropes. A trip to some of these romantic and sacred places can be strenuous. Cirilo takes us along with him. According to the ancient Tzolkin calendar, today is Aq'ab'aal 13, the holiday of the solar new year. For the candidates to the priesthood, this is the second-to-last altar, and it is located in the cave of Chicoy in the misty forests near Cobán. A black maw gapes in a cliff, a sheer and slippery downward climb sometimes secured by ropes, into smoky darkness. Not until you are at the bottom do you realize that you are standing inside a huge underground dome as high as a gothic cathedral. The group consists of thirty people who wish to be initiated into the Maya rites, including some foreigners. All of them have brought offerings—incense pellets, candles, clear hard liquor, and flowers. Sugar is strewn onto the sooty ground in the shape of a white cross within a circle, and then the offerings for the gods are layered atop. The Maya cross marks the four corners of the universe and symbolizes the four elements: fire, water, air, and earth. Cirilo lights the sacred fire; dense smoke darkens the entrance to the cave. The master recites incantations and chants an ancient song. The fire also serves as an oracle: The priest can interpret the future based on the shape of the flames.

Then Cirilo launches into a political and historical discourse, speaks of the suffering of the Maya people. He describes their persecution by the Spaniards and the Church, when the Maya and their shamans were forever being demonized as infidel sorcerers. "The Church taught us to hate, but our religion survived underground for five hundred years. The scientists say the Maya have disappeared, but that is not true. We're still here. Our wisdom is not to be found in schools, we got it from our father Sun." However, according to an ancient prophecy found in the Popol Vuh, the Maya bible, a period of opening and liberation has now begun, and better times are ahead. There are indications for this like the new Guatemalan Peace Treaty or the Nobel Peace Prize granted to the Quiché Maya Rigoberta Menchú-Tum in 1992. "We no longer have to hide our religion," Cirilo shouts into the darkness. "We deserve our human rights, we are the Maya, and we have survived."

Cirilo Pérez Oxlaj and his wife. Arcadia. live on a farm in Totonicapán. Cirilo is a Maya elder and a respected priest: he is also a political force in the battle for human rights.

Smoke and incense waft from an underground cave deep in the mountains in the Sierra de Chamá. A Maya woman has just attended a ceremony at the holy place.

On the bottom of a deep cave a group of worshipers lights hundreds of candles in the darkness, preparing the holy site for the solemn celebrations of the Maya New Year.

Maestro Cirilo
prepares to light
a pyre, which was
carefully built in
a circle from incense,
candles, herbs, and
aromatic wood. Then
the maestro leads
his followers through
a fireside chant and
recitations from
the holy books
of the Maya.

The priest prays to his gods at a natural altar of volcanic rock. He then embarks on a political discourse, speaking of the suffering of his people and the hopes for a better future. His voice reverberates from the black walls of the cavern.

59

On Good Friday a group of village elders kneels under the cross in the ruined church of San Andrés Sajcabajá. The ceremony blends Catholic and Mayan elements where Ave Marias are mixed with sugarcane liquor to concoct a deep religious fervor.

61

A procession of *penitentes* moves slowly through the sun-drenched streets of San Andrés Sajcabajá. Some carry cactus branches on bare backs on Good Friday, while others shuffle down the dusty roads in leg irons and on their knees. Pain brings honor to the volunteers.

A penitent carrying a crown of thorns and a spiny cactus limb stops in a roadside chapel on his way through town. His face is covered with a cloth and he is helped and guided by a handler. The grueling procession lasts for half a day.

Another Easter procession parades through the town of Jocotenango. Men in black are engulfed by clouds of incense. They burn copal resin, which has been used since the days of the ancient Maya.

The *Maximón* is a strange and powerful saint, half Mayan idol, half the apostle Judas. Once a year he is on display in the town square of San Jorge de la Laguna. The wooden figurine is dressed in the finest clothes and receives offerings of bread, cigars, and plenty of hard liquor.

At the rim of a deep gorge, hundreds of revelers have assembled to celebrate the Maya New Year. The exact date of that festive day is determined by the complex mathematics of the ancient Tzolkin calendar.

After the holy fires had been lit, a chicken was sacrificed to appease the gods through its blood. Priests stand high on a rock. Curtains of smoke make them vanish and reappear.

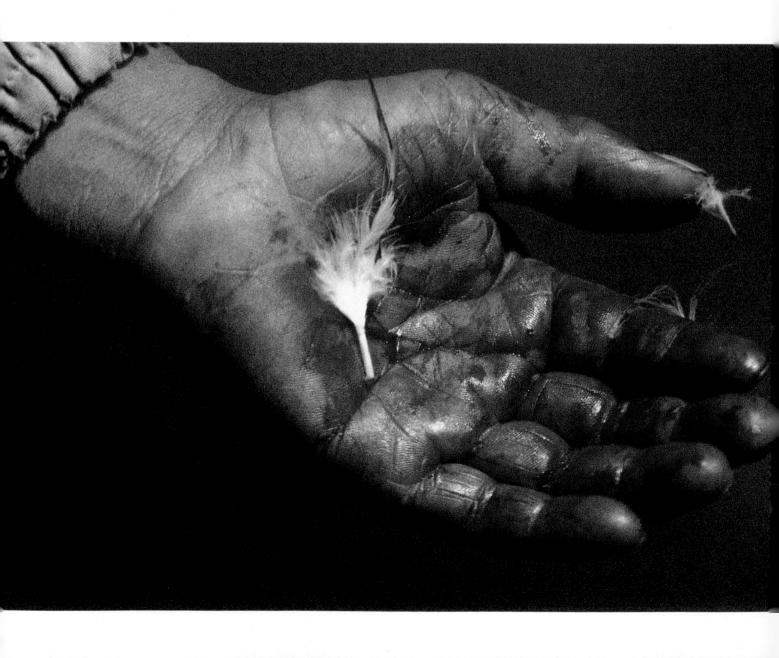

The Maya venerated the cross as a powerful symbol for the layout of their world long before Catholic missionaries began to indoctrinate them to the meaning of the Christian emblem.

Two women are being solemnly ordained by a Maya elder on a mountain near San Francisco El Alto. They have been through months of training and will now go back to their villages as respected shamans. healers. and priests.

On the slopes of the Lacandón volcano in the misty rain forest of the Selva de las Nubes we had visited Guatemala's last guerrilla fighters. They had embraced us cordially, called out *Bienvenidos compañeros!* ("Welcome comrades"), and immediately invited us for corn tamales, which, wrapped in green leaves, were steaming in a huge kettle on the campfire. They insisted that they were glad the war was finally over. They were eager to return to their families. Back to what they called the "legal life." This was a group of 140 disciplined young people, including an astonishing number of girls. They wore clean uniforms, slept in little tents, and each had an Uzi or Kalashnikov slung over his or her shoulder at all times, even when drawing water or collecting wood in the valley below, because they never knew if the cease-fire would really hold. After the meal, they sat down in a jungle clearing, and on a big blackboard an officer wrote words like "class struggle" and "exploitation," but also "human rights" and "amnesty." Although they all looked alert and intelligent, some of them had trouble following the civics lesson. They could not read. They had never needed that skill as long as they were guerrilla fighters. Now they learned to write in their school notebooks with leaden hands, slowly and clumsily, and the girls giggled.

One of them had a long black braid and quick eyes; she said she was nineteen and she was called Alejandra, but that was her war name, not her civilian name. Her Spanish was good even though she was a Cakchiquel Maya. "My first battle was in the town of Santa María de Jesús," she said. "The army sent a tank against us. We didn't stand a chance with our rifles." Alejandra's boyfriend was now working with the mine-detonation unit on the volcano up above. "That experience will come in handy in his new occupation, he wants to become an electrician," Alejandra said. "My father was in the guerrilla movement too. When he got killed, I became a freedom fighter. I saw how badly women are treated in our society. I had to do something." We meet Alejandra once more, now in July. She has had to surrender her beloved old AK-7 rifle to the UN command and now lives in a camp on the outskirts of Quezaltenango. When we find the former rebel, she is frying potatoes in a dark passageway in front of her bunk. She is wearing jeans and a T-shirt instead of the attractive uniform. She has just come back from a course in retail management. Everything here looks dingy and a little bleak. Does she ever wish she could go back to the camp in the misty forest? "No, not really," she says bravely. "Our fight is still going on, only with different means." Didn't the guerrilla movement finally lose the

Alejandra. nineteen. is living out her last days as a guerrilla fighter in a jungle camp. She is a devout Marxist and will have problems adjusting to the normal life of her hometown.

How can a brave rebel be transformed into a good citizen?
For years the guerrilla fighters lived a perilous life
in the jungle. Now they have to adapt
to the unknown hazards of civilian existence.

OUT OF THE WOODS

war? "Oh, no, not at all. We've achieved a great deal. Otherwise we would never have gotten the rights we've got now. Without the guerrilla there would have been no progress, no justice."

It had been the incredible misfortune of the Maya natives to be caught—uninvolved and innocently—in the crossfire when the first rebels of the Marxist-Leninist resistance went underground in the early 1960s. Earlier, in 1954, with massive support from the CIA, the Guatemalan military had staged a coup and ousted President Arbenz, a democratically elected liberal. To the benefit of the large landowners and the United States' United Fruit Company, the coup annihilated most social and land reforms and ignited a vicious reign of terror. The Marxist rebels, most of them renegade officers, were based in the mountains and the rain forest. They looted the Indians' fields, forced the Maya to stash away weapons, extorted information, and bullied the poor—precisely those proletarians in whose name they had set out to carry the revolution all the way to the capital, following the Cuban example. Almost as soon as the guerrilla fighters had left, the soldiers came into the villages. They too demanded information and started looting, but they were much worse— torturing, raping, and killing with modern weapons they had just gotten from the United States. Some of the Indians joined the guerrilla movement. But many young

A jungle classroom
is used to teach
reading, writing,
and math to the
guerrilleros who did
not have too much use
for such mundane
skills. The rifle was
closer to their hearts
than the pen.

Peace brings boredom
to the fighters in the
camp but also visits
from family and children
whom many had not
seen for years. It was
dangerous, even suicidal,
to visit their hometowns,
where police or
informers could have
spotted the outcasts.

A surprising number of young girls had joined the guerrilla movement. Life and love was free-spirited in the camps. where perfecting new writing skills now seems to be the greatest challenge for a courageous fighter. Corn tamales wrapped in green leaves were a delicacy at lunchtime.

men were kidnapped into the military. Grabbed from the road and thrown into trucks, they were simply renamed "recruits." Often they were forced to fight their own people. Maya against Maya—it was always the Indians who were being murdered or driven off the very land for which they had broken their backs all these years to make arable. Hundreds of thousands of them were forced to flee to Mexico or to remote hideouts ever higher up in the mountains.

"The Indians weren't considered people," explains Ronalth Ochaeta, director of the Bureau for Human Rights at the archdiocese in Guatemala City. "The military's propaganda had reduced them to the level of animals and vermin, so there were no scruples when it came to killing them. Besides, the Indians had become pesky, they had started organizing in the CUC, the agricultural workers' union. The international media have never picked up on all that. During the eighties they concentrated exclusively on Nicaragua and Chile. This here is a forgotten war." The genocide of the Maya people in the late 1970s and 1980s, very convenient for the governments of Generals Lucas García and Ríos Montt, thus happened outside the scope of public and international opinion. Since the peace treaty of December 1996, political crimes and war crimes can be investigated but not prosecuted. Only human rights violations can be brought before the courts. "We want to help to clear up the past as long as we are able to do so," Ochaeta says. "We still have a budget of almost a million dollars a year; 41 percent of our money, $414,000 to be exact, came from Germany. But we are not getting a single centavo from the U.S."

A dangerous but romantic life in the jungles ended under the tin roofs of the U.N.-controlled transition camp. Here the rebels had to give up their cherished weapons, and they began to understand that today Che Guevara is nothing but a T-shirt hero.

Commandante Neri, the last commander of the rebel group Las Abejas, stands in pouring rain under the tin roof of a clapboard house in the UN controlled demilitarization camp. Neri, a veteran of sixteen years in the guerrilla, has overseen the transformation of his comrades from rebels to burghers. "It was not easy to keep their enthusiasm alive, to make them understand that you can still be a good Marxist even in a capitalist society." Some of them have already found jobs at security firms—a booming business in a country that has become the world leader in the number of abductions of wealthy people for ransom money. Suddenly Commandante Neri jumps up and runs through the driving rain to catch his bus to Quezaltenango. There he will work as a teacher, he will have a family, and he will use a gun only occasionally—for hunting.

The ex-guerrillas are not welcomed everywhere. There have been problems, even some violence in the workplace. But according to a 1997 independent poll, 84 percent of Guatemalans said that the military violates human rights, while only 36 percent think that the URNG guerrillas have done so; 76 percent think that the military should be drastically reduced or abolished altogether; 83 percent of Guatemalans polled believe that if the army did not exist, there would be less violence in their country, and 69 percent are convinced that when a member of the military commits a crime he does not get punished. And 95 percent of the Guatemalan women polled declared that they have no trust in the armed forces whatsoever.

During Easter celebrations young men dressed as Roman soldiers carry a heavy float through a dusty town with the very Catholic name of Santa María de Jesús.

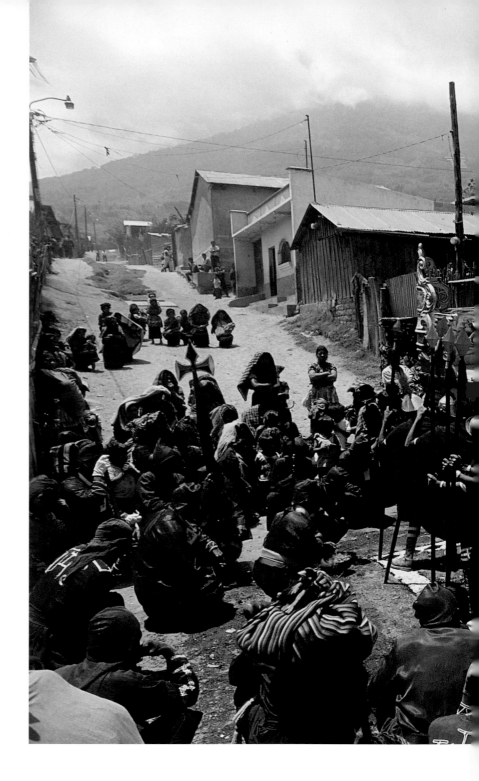

There is always something to celebrate somewhere in Guatemala. A patron saint, a market day, or just an important date on the Maya calendar.

A FESTIVAL A DAY

They say the story is true: Three American social workers witnessed a procession on Good Friday in a remote village in the Guatemalan highlands. When the heavy wooden statue of the Virgin Mary was carried from the church on the shoulders of the members of the *cofradía*, one man, probably drunk, stumbled and fell. The whole float came down, the Madonna capsized, and the Americans saw that the wooden figure was in fact hollow and had sheltered an ancient Mayan stone idol. The gringos were chased from the village, but they are sure that the believers had never really meant to carry the mother of God around town but instead the old Mayan god Chac. In fact this widely used practice of religious deception has a Spanish name: *santos panzones*, the holy bellies.

The Baile de la Conquista,
a masked dance that purports
to celebrate the Spanish
conquest, actually mocks the
invaders and their white
faces. The dance may look
and sound monotonous
to the outsider, but it is
watched with fascination
by the villagers, even
the very young ones.

A small Ferris wheel, which is still moved around by hand, is an attraction at this fiesta in San Francisco El Alto. The simple pleasures of a festive day attract visitors from faraway towns.

Getting drunk at the fiesta is half the fun for the men. Like most indigenous people, the Maya have little tolerance for alcohol. The wives and children wait patiently until their husbands or fathers have sobered enough to be guided home safely.

The Tiger dancers at
Panajachel take a beer
break at the local tienda.
With good sense for color
coordination a lady
at Santiago Atitlán enjoys
a purple Popsicle.

The *Maximón* of Santiago Atitlán gets dressed in silk scarves and a large hat and is given a big cigar for his procession on Easter Saturday. He is carried past the church, where he greets his arch rivals, the Christian saints, and is then brought into his own chapel.

The Maya observe
and conserve their
customs. A bride
is tied to the neck of
her groom; sacred
skulls, believed to be
of ancient kings,
are kissed and
venerated in the
Petén by the Itzá
Maya; and an elder
uses olive branches
for a festive crown
in Santa María de
Jesús.

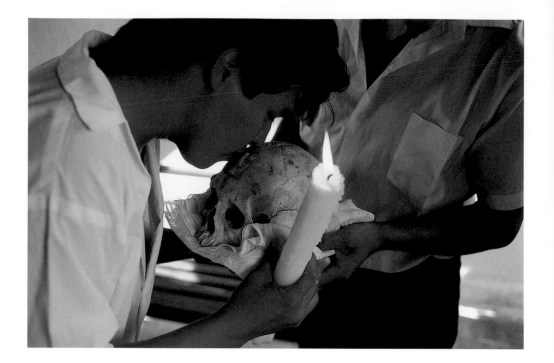

Even saints have to fight for their space in traffic when a procession winds its way through the congested streets of Chichicastenango.

The women of
San Francisco
El Alto celebrate
the festival of
their patron
saint with flow-
ers, candles, and
a procession
that lasts for a
full day.

Copán, one of the most romantic Maya ruins, lies just across the border in Honduras. The giant head of an old man, a *pauahtun* watches over classic art and architecture. The great hieroglyphic stairway is kept clean by a guard with a natural broom.

The secrets of the ancient Maya are being unearthed
and interpreted at breakneck speed. But there is
always something else, another hidden temple
to be excavated, another enigma to be solved.

DIGS

The ruins of Uaxactún lie only a short distance north of the tourist hub of Tikal in the Petén region. Visitors rarely come this way, and many structures are still hidden, dormant and unexplored, under mounds of jungle growth.

A young high school teacher from Guatemala meets one of his forefathers in the ruined city of Copán. There is a new curiosity among the educated Maya to explore their past and to come to grips with their own roots.

Professor Linda Schele from Austin, Texas, who died in 1998, was instrumental in decoding the Maya hieroglyphs. She interpreted a text at Copán and taught young Maya the use of their own ancient language.

The Mayan king "Eighteen Rabbit," depicted in this stela, ruled Copán from A.D. 695 for forty-three years. A young margay, a relative of the ocelot, roams the ruins of Tikal.

Diane and Arlen Chase, professors of anthropology from Orlando, Florida, have been excavating the site of Caracol in Belize for the past five years. They found this burial chamber inside Caana, the main pyramid.

On Friday, May 7, 1993, around 4:00 P.M., Professor Arlen Chase is on his knees way down in B-20, sweeping some loose soil off the bottom. B-20 is a deep shaft the archaeologists have dug down from the plaza on top of the big pyramid named Caana at the Caracol site, deep in the rain forest of Belize. Arlen spots a fine crack between two large square stone slabs. After sweeping more rubble aside, he is quite certain that he is looking at the capstones of a burial chamber.

Lying on his belly he tries to peer through one crack while shining a light through another. He stares down into a deep chamber and can make out a wide red stripe on one wall, a lot of rubble, and even the green-and-red rim of a half-buried ceramic vase. He sinks a tape measure down through the slit and measures three meters to the bottom. "Holy shit—that's quite something!" His wife, Diane Chase, also takes a long look. Then, brushing off the dirt from her jeans, she reaches for the walkie-talkie: "Caana to lab! Maureen, is this you? Turn down the volume so not everybody will hear this. Okay—Maureen, is the fridge working at all?" "Let me check," the voice crackles back. "Yea, kind of medium cool." "Okay, now listen: in that box under our beds there are four bottles of bubbly. Put them in the fridge for tonight. But don't tell anybody yet!"

Arlen explains that the new chamber is located exactly behind two tombs that had been looted by grave robbers ten years ago on the east side of the pyramid. "This is the tomb they missed. We have been looking for it for a couple of years. This is sensational. I think it's really important. This must be a very old chamber, probably early classic." Arlen is excited and proud. The Chases have been hoping for such a success for a long time. They have spent eight summers with their students at the site. They invested hard work and much routine. They've had small finds, shards and bones, but this is a major breakthrough. It will help with fund-raising for the next season, when they are back home at the University of Central Florida in Orlando. Lukewarm champagne is poured for everyone after a meal of chicken and beans this evening.

For the next four days the Chases are very busy. The area around B-20 has to be cleaned and secured with concrete. Diane takes measurements and makes sketches. Mundane problems need solutions. Wednesday they have to drive to the bank in town. The workers have to get paid. The cook has started some hanky-panky with a Maya worker, so another man has gotten pretty mad. The cook has to go. But who will prepare the meals for the workers now? A student comes back from San Ignacio after some minor surgery. She has contracted lice in the hospital. Diane gets on the radio trying to locate a special shampoo. Now the whole of Belize can listen in and learn that they have lice at Caracol. Finally on Thursday at seven in the morning the Chases leave camp to climb up to the plaza on Caana. As usual, Arlen carries his coffee mug. Two workers lift one of the capstones and clear the entrance to the tomb. A rope ladder is lowered, and Diane squeezes herself through the opening, down into the dark corbel vault. Arlen follows, panting. The morning is hot and the air in the

HOW A MAYAN KING WAS DISCOVERED IN CARACOL (OR WAS IT A QUEEN?)

chamber is stale and sticky. The Chases measure the grave. It is exactly 3.3 meters high; they calculate 19.2 cubic meters of volume—an unusually big chamber, the second largest in Caracol. One has to be careful down in the dusty hole. It's easy to crush an object in the rubble underfoot. Even touching a crumbling wall may destroy information. Arlen stares at the dark red stripe on the wall for a long time. He thinks he can see some rough dark lines, hastily brushed onto the wall with charcoal. He says he can probably decipher the "long count" date as 9.5.3.2. Later at night his laptop translates this into the Gregorian calendar date of A.D. 537. But Arlen is not totally sure of what he has read.

Friday is the day of dirt moving. Bucket after bucket is filled by the Chases with damp soil and rocks. Juan, a worker, stands outside and pulls the heavy loads out into the sunlight. Josh and Kirk, students from Orlando, dump everything onto a large sieve and pick out small fragments: bone, obsidian, jade, ceramic shards, spines of a stingray, stucco fragments, and arrow tips, which are small and sharp as a knife. Everything is sorted and put into plastic bags. Arlen finds a large Spondylus shell. "A clear sign of an important personality," he says. "This is a rare shell, and it must have come all the way from the Pacific."

On Sunday the Chases work a full day inside the tomb. With a spoon, a toothpick, brushes, and bare hands they clear dirt from objects. Diane carefully lifts a fine vase from one corner. It is totally intact and has black geometric bands on a red background. When all debris is cleared out the remains of a skeleton become visible on the smooth ground. Leg bones, a hint of an arm with a hand, fragments of a skull. Some teeth have holes drilled into them and are filled with specks of jade. Around noon Diane brushes a small green splinter from the floor. It gets bigger as she goes on, and we recognize a jade pendant of strong green color about two by three centimeters. Only when Arlen turns it around can he see the nicely carved male figure on the other side. Not far from it there is a handful of spindle whirls, small round pieces of ceramic with a hole in the middle. They had been used as weights to hold down wool threads during spinning or weaving.

Arlen has not made any progress with the interpretation of the date. The problem is that if the date of death is really the year 537, then the skeleton cannot be that of a ruler. The precise dates of the kings of Caracol are known from a stela that was found here and is now in the Philadelphia museum. This date does not fit the list. On the other hand, the large size of the tomb, the Spondylus shell, the jade pendant, all point toward an important personality. Or maybe this was not a king but a queen, after all? The bones have deteriorated too much. Not even Diane, who has taken courses in anatomy, can say if she is looking at a man or a woman. They want to send bone fragments back to Orlando for DNA analysis just to make sure.

From above, looking down into the deep chamber, one can see a faint dark contour around the bones. For 1,450 years a human being has slowly oozed into the soil. Maybe that dark patch we are looking at is the aura of a king? The soul of a queen?

Arlen Chase peers into a shaft that leads into a newly found tomb in the pyramid. A red-and-black vase was among the finds as well as shards and bone fragments, which are carefully sorted and numbered by the students.

Arlen Chase tries to
read a red glyph
on the wall of an
underground
chamber, then he
and his wife brush
away soil from the
remains of a Mayan
dignitary. A small
jade figurine is
found among
the rubble.

The ancient Maya had never invented the wheel.
Sometimes it seems as if the modern Maya
have still not heard about it.
Everywhere in the highlands men, women, and children
carry heavy loads on their backs—firewood,
produce in baskets, cement sacks, even live animals.

THE HUMAN MULE

Two hours down
into the valley
in early morning.
Three hours back to
the house at night,
uphill, with
a heavy load and
the kid and the
sheep—just to
get the wood to
cook the meal and
to keep warm for
one more night.

Beams for construction
or reeds for basket
weaving—almost
everything can be
transported on the backs
of men. Anthropologists
have found ugly
deformations in the
skeletons of most Maya.

A butcher
in Antigua
Guatemala
carries half
a cow from
a van to his store.

128

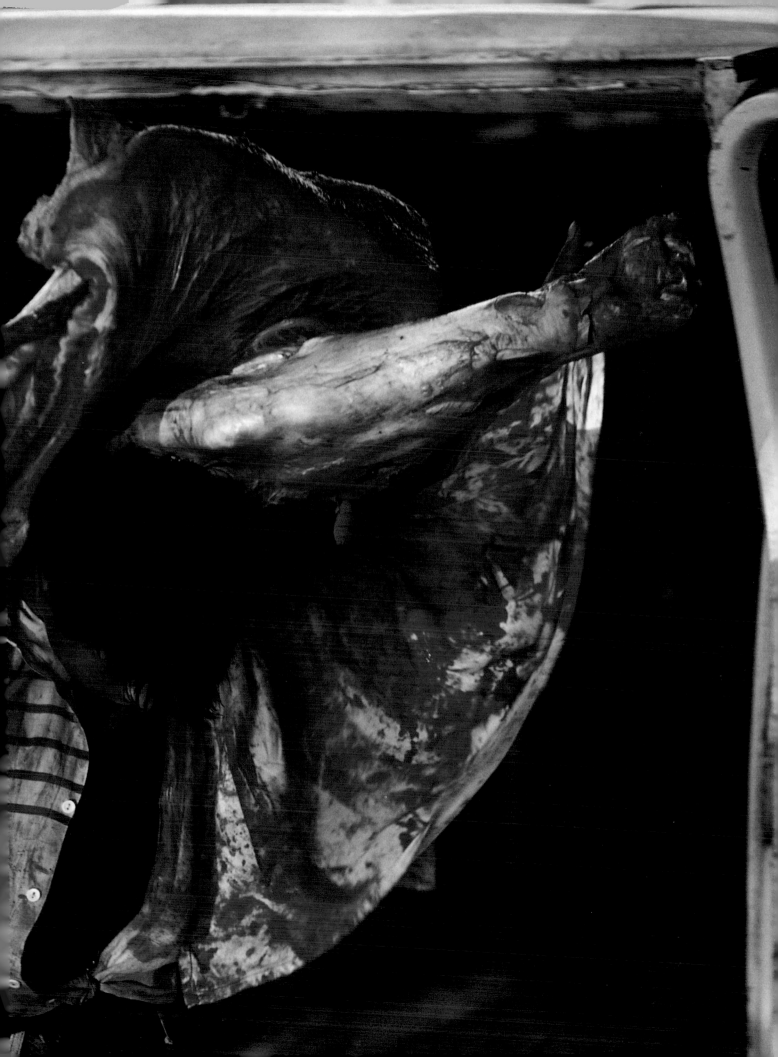

Women in black
carry a heavy, holy
load—the statue of
Jesus—in the Easter
procession at Antigua
Guatemala. Live
turkeys are brought to
the animal market in
large round baskets.

A father and
his son carry
bundles of fresh
radishes through
the morning
fog to the
market in Zunil.

PROMISES AND PERILS

Dressed up as
a Ninja Turtle, a
little boy stands
in a bodega
that in itself
is a monument
to plastic culture.

The Maya have weathered the horrors of a thirty-six-year war
and five hundred years of religious persecution.
Now they have to learn to survive peace.
Will they be able to resist the lures of capitalism
and pop culture, just as they have struggled to
preserve their lives and their indigenous identity?

Families who visit
relatives' graves
on the Day of the
Dead are convinced
that Coca-Cola is
better than manna.
A green carousel
monster is welcomed
as a sign of modern
times, just as is the
cartoon shirt of
the Jesus peddler.

Heavenly signals in Jocotenango: The Pietá passes satellite dishes of Guatel, the telephone company. Now, after peace has been made, new technology comes to even the remotest villages.

Modern times bring
modern advertising.
A dentist in Chajul
makes his message
clear: Somewhat like
the computer center,
he promises to improve
the Mayabite. A
cynical billboard near
Chichicastenango
tries to reposition
the military as friend
of the Indios, trying
to make them forget
the atrocities of the war.

Now there is Disney in Mayaland, also a colorful potency tonic and the freakish skulls on a sweatshirt: Pop culture has arrived in postwar Guatemala.

The bikini girl cooling it on a beer bottle must appear rather alien to the local women, but it may mean a lot to the truckers who pass through the beautiful highland scenery above Quezaltenango.

Like every photographer's wife, Eva Windmöller had to suffer through years of talk and planning while my book project took shape. She also gave the best advice in the editing of my texts and was, as usual, the most demanding critic of my photographs.

Christine Kruchen not only worked perfectly as a sensitive interpreter, she also did invaluable research in Guatemala. Through her I met the most significant characters in this book and learned about important events.

Susanne Baumgartner added professionalism and immaculate taste to my own clumsy attempts to lay out the pages of this book.

I owe heartfelt thanks to Cirilo Pérez Oxlaj, the Maya priest, who allowed me to see and photograph things that had not been photographed before. He also taught me a lot about his religion and culture.

I admire the teams of anthropologists who have shouldered the grisly task of exhuming the victims of the war and who let me observe them and their work.

My deepest admiration is for the Maya people, especially the brave women who have not only survived a holocaust but are now courageous enough to rebuild their lives, feed their families, and preserve their values.

Thomas Hoepker

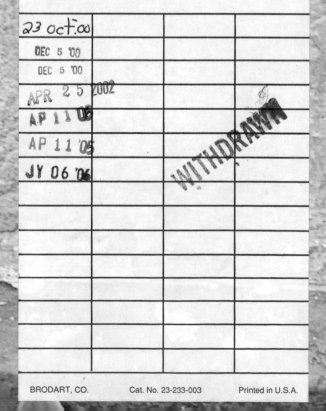

Date Due

23 Oct.'00			
DEC 5 '00			
DEC 5 '00			
APR 2 5 2002			
AP 11 '05			WITHDRAWN
AP 11 '05			
JY 06 '06			